Rain forest

Sarah Levete

Crabtree Publishing
crabtreebooks.com

Author: Sarah Levete

Editors: Kathy Middleton
Crystal Sikkens

Project coordinator: Kathy Middleton

Production coordinator: Ken Wright

Prepress technicians: Ken Wright
Margaret Amy Salter

Photographs

Dreamstime: Shariff Che' Lah: page 9; Ryszard Laskowski: page 14; Michael Lynch: page 13; Xiaobin Qiu: pages 3, 12; Steveheap: page 7; Swisshippo: page 4; Lawrence Wee: page 19
Shutterstock: cover; 7877074640: pages 1, 11; Nina B: page 20; Todd Boland: page 21; Steve Bower: page 16; Joseph Calev: page 6; Hannamariah: page 18; Giancarlo Liguori: page 5; Dr. Morley Read: pages 8, 15; Chai Kian Shin: page 17; Worldswildlifewonders: page 10

Library and Archives Canada Cataloguing in Publication

Levete, Sarah
Rain forest / Sarah Levete.

(Crabtree connections)
Includes index.
ISBN 978-0-7787-7843-1 (bound).--ISBN 978-0-7787-7865-3 (pbk.)

1. Rain forest ecology--Juvenile literature. 2. Rain forests--Juvenile literature. I. Title. II. Series: Crabtree connections

QH541.5.R27L49 2011 j577.7'27 C2011-900602-2

Library of Congress Cataloging-in-Publication Data

Levete, Sarah.
Rain forest / Sarah Levete.
p. cm. -- (Crabtree connections)
Includes index.
ISBN 978-0-7787-7865-3 (pbk. : alk. paper) -- ISBN 978-0-7787-7843-1 (reinforced library binding : alk. paper)
1. Rain forest ecology--Juvenile literature. 2. Rain forests--Juvenile literature. I. Title. II. Series.

QH541.5.R27L475 2012
577.34--dc22

2011001338

Crabtree Publishing Company

www.crabtreebooks.com 1-800-387-7650

Printed in Canada/052024/CPC20240502

Published in Canada
Crabtree Publishing
616 Welland Avenue
St. Catharines, ON
L2M 5V6

Published in the United States
Crabtree Publishing
347 Fifth Ave
Suite 1402-145
New York, NY 10016

Contents

Rain Forest

Many animals, plants, and trees are found in **rain forests**. Some are beautiful; some are strange.

Amazing animals

Bright green lizards called geckos live in rain forests. They have sticky **toe pads** to help them hold on tight as they climb up tall rainforest trees.

Hot and wet

Tropical rain forests are found in hot parts of the world. It rains most days in these forests.

The gecko gobbles up insects.

Tall Trees

Animals live in every part of the rain forest, from the forest floor to the top of the trees. Only a few, such as birds, can reach the tallest trees.

High and low

The scarlet macaw swoops up to the sunny treetops to build its nest. Larger animals make homes on the forest floor.

The macaw has beautiful, bright feathers.

Wobble, wobble!

People who study rainforest animals cross the treetops on rope bridges that sway.

Bug Alert

The rain forest buzzes with insects. Some, such as ants, help clean up the rain forest by eating dead leaves and animals.

Tiny killers!

Hundreds of **army ants** march together, stinging anything in their path. These tiny crawlers can sting a snake to death.

Army ants have a deadly sting.

Important insects

Dragonflies spread **seeds** when they land on flowers. The seeds grow into new plants.

Tree House

Monkeys live high up in the trees. They make a lot of noise, calling out to each other as they leap around.

Hang on!

Spider monkeys have strong tails to help them swing between branches. They grab tasty fruit with their long arms as they swing from tree to tree.

Monkeys are fantastic climbers.

Upside down!

Sloths sleep hanging upside down from the rainforest trees!

In the Air

During the day, colorful birds glide through the treetops and peck at fruit. At night, bats flap and swoop around in the dark.

Beaky eater

The toucan makes its home in small holes in rainforest trees. Its tough beak is perfect for breaking open hard nuts.

Toucans have very bright, strong beaks.

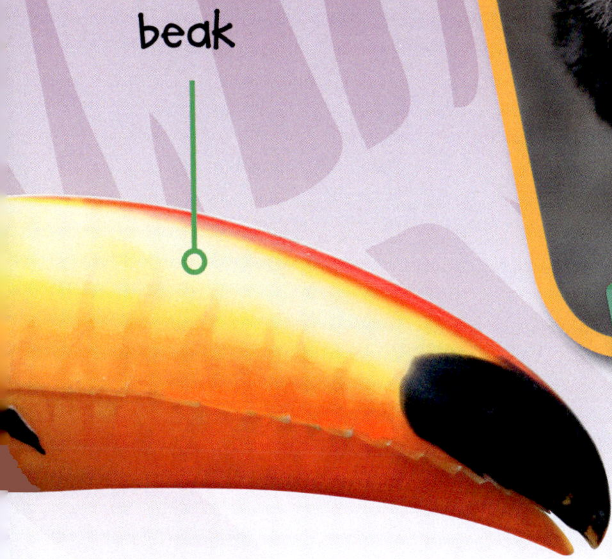

Bloodsucker

Vampire bats use their sharp teeth to bite animals. Then they slurp up their blood. Yuck!

Splash!

Long, winding rivers flow through rain forests. These are home to many animals, such as capybaras.

Water home

Capybaras graze on grass that grows at the edge of rivers. If cabybaras are in danger, they just swim into the river using their **webbed** feet.

Capybaras eat their own poop!

Snap!

Crocodiles rest in river water until they spot a tasty animal to snap up and swallow.

Plant World

Plants and flowers grow everywhere in the rain forest. Insects land on them, and frogs even live in them.

Home, sweet home

Frogs live inside brightly colored plants called bromeliads. The plant's big leaves fill up with rainwater to make a perfect swimming pool for rainforest tree frogs.

Hungry plant

The pitcher plant traps small animals and insects before eating them up!

Tree frogs lay eggs in plants.

Danger!

Rainforest animals work hard to stay alive and find food. Some are fierce **hunters**; others use color to stay safe.

Deadly

The boa constrictor snake slides along tree branches and the rainforest floor, hunting for food. When it finds **prey** to eat, it squeezes it to death before swallowing it whole!

I'm warning you

The bright markings on its wings warn enemies that this butterfly is **poisonous**.

marking

This snake is as long as two **adult** people.

Our Home

Local people have lived in the rain forests for many years. They live in houses they have built.

Living here safely

Rainforest people know which plants and animals can be harmful and which are safe to eat. They also look after the rain forest.

Rainforest people make clothes from plants and feathers.

Pretty good

This pretty pink plant is used to make **medicine.**

Glossary

adult Fully grown

army ants Type of ant that has a poisonous sting

hunters Animals that look for other animals to eat

medicine Something that makes people feel better if they are sick

poisonous Harmful if eaten or touched

prey Animals hunted by other animals for food

rain forests Thick forests where it rains most days

seeds Parts of a plant that can grow into other new plants

sloths Furry animals with very long claws that live in rainforest trees

toe pads Sticky pads on an animal's feet that stick to the surface it is climbing on

tropical Parts of the world where the weather is hot and wet all year round

webbed Covered by a flap of skin to help animals swim

Further Reading

Web Sites

Discover more about rain forests, the animals and plants that live there, and how much rain falls on there at:
www.enchantedlearning.com/subjects/rainforest

Find out more about rain forests and the animals that live there at this interactive encyclopedia:
www.globio.org/glossopedia/article.aspx?art_id=6

Books

A Rainforest Habitat (Introducing Habitats)
by Molly Aloian and Bobbie Kalman,
Crabtree Publishing (2007).

Tangled in the Rainforest (Science to the Rescue)
by Gerry Bailey,
Crabtree Publishing (2014).

Exploring the Rainforest Treetops with a Scientist
by Judith Williams,
Enslow (2004).

Index